Y0500 9724

S0-BUD-735

NO LONGER THE PROPERTY OF
WICHITA PUBLIC LIBRARY

wd 12-11-03
JHP

SCORNFUL SIMKIN

Adapted from Chaucer's *The Reeve's Tale*

Retold and illustrated by

LEE LORENZ

Prentice-Hall, Inc. / Englewood Cliffs, New Jersey

For Nicholas

Copyright © 1980 by Lee Lorenz
All rights reserved. No part of this book may be
reproduced in any form or by any means, except for
the inclusion of brief quotations in a review,
without permission in writing from the publisher.
Printed in the United States of America   J

Prentice-Hall International, Inc., London
Prentice-Hall of Australia, Pty. Ltd., North Sydney
Prentice-Hall of Canada, Ltd., Toronto
Prentice-Hall of India Private Ltd., New Delhi
Prentice-Hall of Japan, Inc., Tokyo
Prentice-Hall of Southeast Asia Pte. Ltd., Singapore
Whitehall Books Limited, Wellington, New Zealand

Library of Congress Cataloging in Publication Data
Lorenz, Lee.   Scornful Simkin.
A retelling of Chaucer's *The Reeve's Tale*
SUMMARY: A miller who cheats his customers
gets his comeuppance from two bright young students.
   [1. Millers—Fiction] I. Title.
PZ7.L884Sc   [E]   80-15785   ISBN 0-13-796664-4

Long ago, near the town of Trumpington, there lived a miller named Simkin.

He had a black beard, a crooked nose and a head as bald as a melon.

Because of his terrible temper and sharp tongue, he was called "Scornful Simkin."

Simkin was a thief. When people brought him
wheat to be ground into flour to make bread, he
always took some for himself.

And when Simkin played cards, he always cheated.

Everyone knew what a scoundrel he was, but no one dared to challenge him for fear of his life.

Simkin had a wife and a baby son still in the cradle. His wife was as vain as he was mean. On Sundays, the two of them would leave the baby with a nurse, put on their finest clothes and strut around the town like peacocks. Simkin led the way wearing scarlet stockings to match his wife's gown. They were a comic sight, indeed!

Of all Simkin's customers, the nearby University at Cambridge was the most important.

One day, when he was grinding wheat for the University, Simkin felt especially greedy, and decided to steal even more flour than usual.

This time, however, he went too far. When the flour was weighed, the dean discovered the theft. He went straight to Simkin and demanded that he return the stolen flour.

WICHITA PUBLIC LIBRARY

Simkin got very angry. "Nobody dares to call me a thief!" he snarled, grabbing the poor dean by the beard and shaking him. "Your scales must be wrong!"

"Per-per-perhaps they are," stuttered the fearful dean.

He quickly jumped back on his horse and rode
away.

Now, studying at Cambridge were two bright young lads named Alan and John. They were full of high spirits and always looking for adventure. So, the next time the University needed flour, the dean asked them to deliver the wheat to the miller.

"See to it that Simkin doesn't cheat us again. This is his last chance!"

"Don't worry, sir," boasted John. "That rascal Simkin will never outwit us." And, loading the wheat onto an old nag, they rode off to the mill.

When they arrived, they asked Simkin if they could watch the grain being ground into flour.

"We are eager to learn from a master-miller," said Alan. Simkin agreed and led them into the mill.

"I'll watch the hopper to see how the wheat goes in," said John.

"And I'll watch the trough to see the flour come out," said Alan. "Perhaps we will learn something."

"Indeed you will," thought Simkin. And while they were watching the grinding, he sneaked outside, untied their horse, and chased him away.

When the grinding was done, John and Alan carried the sackful of flour outside.

"By Saint Cuthbert!" exclaimed Simkin, pretending to be surprised. "Your horse is galloping off to the swamp. Hurry, or you'll never catch him." John and Alan dropped the sack and ran after their horse.

When they were out of sight, Simkin emptied half their flour into another sack and carried both sacks into the house. One he left in the kitchen, and the other he handed to his wife, telling her to hide it under the baby's cradle, which always stood at the foot of their bed.

All afternoon, Alan and John chased after their horse back and forth under the blazing sun.

"Run faster," cried John. "If we don't catch him, we'll be the laughing stock of Cambridge when we get back."

"*You* run faster," shouted Alan. "If we don't catch him, we won't be able to go back at all!"

It was sundown before they finally caught their
nag who had fallen into a ditch. Wet and tired,
they returned to the mill and begged Simkin to
give them a bed for the night. "We will pay you
well," said Alan.

"Agreed," answered Simkin, enjoying their mis-
ery.

He said to his wife, "Our friends will join us for supper and stay the night." Then he made up a bed for Alan and John right next to their own.

Simkin's wife prepared a delicious meal of roast goose, sweet potatoes, turnips, cakes and ale. There was enough food for a banquet!

But Simkin and his wife gobbled up everything,
leaving nothing but crumbs for their guests.

After their enormous meal, the miller and his wife went straight to bed. Soon they were snoring like horses. Glancing around the kitchen, Alan spotted the half empty sack of flour lying in a corner. He picked it up.

"That Simkin has stolen our flour and made fools of us as well."

"We'll find it, never fear," said John.

They searched all over the kitchen for the missing flour. Finally, they decided to look in the bedroom.

Prowling around in the dark, Alan came upon the cradle at the foot of Simkin's bed. "What better hiding place! Help me move it," he whispered to John.

They lifted the cradle carefully and carried it to the foot of their own bed.

"Look!" said John. "Here is the other sack!" He picked it up and they headed quickly for the door.

But the sound of their footsteps awoke the
miller's wife. Jumping out of bed, she grabbed a
stick from the corner, and began to swing it
around wildly in the dark. Alan and John hid
behind the door.

At that moment, a moonbeam fell on the cradle. Suddenly a terrible thought came to Simkin's wife. She reached down under the cradle. The sack of flour was gone!

"So they found the flour," she muttered. "Well, getting it out of here is not going to be easy!"

She paused for a moment.

"If the cradle is *there*," she thought, "then *this* must be the bed of those scoundrels."

Swinging the stick as hard as she could, she beat at the hump in the bed. "Take that and that!" she cried.

Much to her surprise, it was Simkin who jumped up, yelling, "Help! Someone's trying to kill me!" And he fell out of bed with a thud. The baby woke up and began to cry. In all the confusion, Alan and John managed to run out.

As they dashed through the kitchen, John
grabbed the other sack.

They ran from the mill and rode back to Cambridge as fast as they could.

Y0500 9724

And so, Scornful Simkin got his just rewards. He received no pay for his work. He lost his best customer, Cambridge University. And he was sorely beaten by his own wife.

This proves the old saying: "He who does evil can expect no good."